An Altar
of Stories
to Liminal
Saints

—·—

Rios de la Luz

Broken River Books

Broken River Books

Edmond, OK 73013

ISBN: 978-1-940885-60-5

For Irma and for my beautiful friend, Pamela K. Santos.
I love you.

CONTENTS

DIRT

The first time Ignacio tasted dirt, he tripped over his shoelaces in front of his Abuela. He was going to greet her with a kiss on her wrinkled cheeks, but he fell instead. With his mouth open to the earth below him, the dirt stuffed itself into his cheeks and sat on his tongue. Ignacio swallowed the dirt and became dizzy with ecstasy. The dirt made him see stars. Ignacio felt like he could taste the entire season of summer in his mouth. The dirt tasted like a thunderstorm and a cyclone. Dangerous, but delicious all the same. He never tasted anything like it. After the dirt, Ignacio tried eating tree bark, moss, dragonfly wings, tiny pebbles, but his palate could never replicate the divine nutrition of dirt.

Ignacio was now an adult and his habit was a simple part of life. He kept baby food jars filled with dirt in his temporary new apartment and in his car. He kept a stash in the glove compartment in case of emergency. He kept small vials with cork stops in his pocket to satiate his cravings throughout the day. In the beginning of summer, his mouth watered at the smell of air conditioners being turned on for the first time.

Dust storms were the best. Ignacio stood out in the harsh winds and let the dirt envelope him and stick to his eyelashes and in between the gaps of his teeth. The crunch of the grit was worth the discomfort.

Ignacio wanted to become an archeologist. He wanted to taste the bones of dinosaurs with a dash of meteor dust and the destruction of prior empires. He had tasted massacres and war. War dirt was bitter and made his belly bloat. Construction work was close enough for now. On job sites, he patted down red dirt with his palms. He made miniature piles and stuck his hands inside them, then he ran his hands through his hair. After hard days of work, sweat dribbled down his face and he could taste the salt and the dirt. The construction crew didn't seem to mind. They'd had worse men to deal with. Men on meth, high as hot air balloons. Men who loved cocaine more than their paychecks. Men who were too drunk to function. Ignacio just had a thing for dirt.

Ignacio had a baby girl on the way, but he was unsure what he could give her as a father, aside from a small stash of money he hid in the hallway linen closet. Baby girl was to be kept a secret. He had another family in a different state. He didn't have the heart to stick around and meet his new baby. He hoped her mother would bestow baby girl with the name "Luna." Ignacio wondered what dirt on different moons and planets tasted like. He wondered if Luna would ever think of him as she felt sand between her toes or as she watched dust devils swirling around on desert roads. No, no. Luna's mother would most likely lie about who he was. She'll say, her daddy was loyal, selfless, and a man who loved God. Lies, establishing an endearing man in the eyes of Luna. This was better than the truth. This was better than nothing.

Five years passed. Ignacio thought about Luna on days when there was an unexplainable small ache in his chest. Faint pain in the depth of his gut. He wanted something miraculous to happen to him. He didn't want money or fame or adoration. He wanted to find meaning in a life he considered mediocre. He took care of his family, he loved them hard, and had a steady job, but then, there was Luna. How could he connect with her after all these years? Telling his wife could ruin their marriage, their stability, how his three children saw him, but he wanted to see Luna, even if only once.

Ignacio started snacking on tree bark and little stones again. He ate flower petals and dead bees. He started looking for holy dirt to consume. One morning, before sunrise, he drove to El Santuario de Chimayo. Ignacio envisioned this chapel in a dream. A pied crow landed on his shoulder and when it opened its mouth, the sound of bell chimes blared out. Ignacio entered the chapel and smelled ancient muds. The dirt was tucked away beside an altar with thousands of offerings from previous visitors. El Pocito, the small pit of dirt, called to Ignacio, and with a tiny silver spoon he dug at the dirt and he tasted religion. He tasted profound hope. He tasted a spiritual awakening. He saw a spirit. She was young, at least three, and playful. She pulled at his shirt and then hid in the pews. Her footsteps echoed inside, but she vanished. He saw Saint Francis surrounded by squirrels and bunnies. A fox screamed at Ignacio. Ignacio reached into its mouth and found a monarch butterfly. Ignacio ate the butterfly and tasted nectars from the jungle. He tasted migration and milkweed. He stumbled out of the chapel and couldn't breathe. He grabbed at his throat. No air was getting in. He tried screaming and coughing, but all his body knew to do was choke. Ignacio collapsed. He ached for air, but nothing gave. He felt something wriggle in his throat. He reached into his mouth and started to pull. It felt like thick hair and electrical wiring. He continued to pull and pull, then tree roots and what looked like giant red slugs of mucus and meat slowly emerged out. Blood poured out of his mouth as he continued to pull at the thing stuck in his throat. When there was nothing left to pull, Ignacio got up, soaked in his blood from his hair down to his toes squishing in their socks. His eyes widened. It was a human heart. A human heart, the size of four giant bags of topsoil on a pallet, quivering in front of him. Ignacio felt the thing and it was beating. It was slick and slimy, like a newborn baby still in its mother's water. He went back into the chapel to ask for help. The priest inside gasped at the sight of bloody Ignacio and whispered that God's work is never done in the name of the father the son and the holy ghost as he walked outside toward the heart to lend a hand.

The priest helped Ignacio lift the heart into a wheelbarrow. The priest, now covered in blood himself, wondered who the heart truly belonged to. Should it go into the core of the earth?

Should it sit in the Vatican like a secret? If this came out of that man, was it rightfully his? The priest decided to pray over it. He asked God to strike him down with crackling lightning as a sign that the heart belonged to the chapel. When he needed an answer, nothing happened. So, he let it go. The heart could travel with the man.

Ignacio called his buddies who lived in Albuquerque. He told them it was too hard to explain, but he needed help transporting something to his daughter in Oregon. Fernando and Lou tagged along on the road trip. Fernando was a construction work friend of four years. Lou met Ignacio when they got into an altercation outside of a strip club. They quickly bonded over being born in Juárez. Their friendship blossomed from there. The giant heart sat in the back of the truck, tied down with bungee cords and adorned in a blue tarp. Most of the road trip was silent, but there were moments when the men talked about the conspiracies they believed in. Ignacio thinks Bigfoot is a ghost, definitely real, but a lost apparition. Fernando believes we are in the matrix. Lou believes Kaiju are real, which made Ignacio and Fernando laugh into tears. At gas stations, children stopped in their tracks to stare at the back of the truck. This confirmed to Ignacio that he was doing right by Luna.

When they got to Oregon, they found themselves in an awkward situation. Ignacio knocked on the door and Luna looked through the peephole, terrified of the stranger outside. His face was a blur and her heart raced in panic. She was alone in the house with the family's chihuahua, Cheeto. Ignacio could sense someone behind the door. He motioned to Fernando and Lou. They carried the heart into the backyard and placed it in the center of the yard, between a bird bath and a lemon tree. Ignacio looked through the sliding glass door. Luna hid in her mom's room, under the bed, praying for the men to go away.

Ignacio's chest ached. He wanted to meet his daughter, but shame took over again. He was too embarrassed to show up all of a sudden, desperate for her acceptance or her love or just an acknowledgment that he exists. He poured a vial of dirt into his mouth and coughed it out immediately because he saw a lanky crooked creature out of the corner of his eye.

Luna wandered out into the living room and slowly tiptoed toward the sliding glass door to the backyard. She got to the door and watched the heart expand and contract as though it was inside someone's chest. Luna could hear something in the heart, whispering to her. She slid the door open and the whispering got louder. The whispers flooded the sound around her. Nothing of clarity, all gibberish in a different tongue and psst psst psst as though she were a cat. She couldn't hear Cheeto growling and barking. She couldn't hear the traffic outside as people honked on their ways home. She couldn't hear her mom get home from work and run to the backyard to scream at her to get away from that thing. Luna touched the heart and heard the earth under her feet cracking. The ground lifted her up. She reached into a slit in the right atrium, the inside was warm and gooey, like honey or sap. She slowly pulled out a photograph. A man she'd never seen before. Her mom grabbed Luna, snatched the photo, wiped away the sticky blood, and brought the photo closer to her face.

It's your dad.

This is a photo of your dad.

For years, the heart is a spectacle in the neighborhood. Year after year, the heart shrinks. People claim it has healing powers. Lucia says she no longer has arthritis. Titi says her knees don't hurt anymore, she does squats as she swears to God. Others say the heart whispers to them and gives them advice. Janet finally got a divorce. Heriberto finally opened his palm reading business. Some people call the heart a trick of the devil. They spit on the curb in front of Luna's house and leave bibles haphazardly strewn across the front yard.

The shrinking heart is now surrounded by marigolds and offerings brought by an influx of visitors. The heart whispers to Luna every night. The heart wants her to sleep inside of it so it can smother her and wring her until there's nothing left. The heart wants to crush her bones and her brain like a reticulated python. The heart wants to hear her organs pop like balloons. The heart whispers that these are all jokes. Plus, Luna's too big now, she can't sleep inside of it anyway. The heart doesn't taunt or threaten Luna as much as it whines and fantasizes about sitting the chest of a man who owns too many tropical birds. Luna gives the heart grace. To the heart's point, it's bored with being a spectacle. The heart's tongue is a mixture of Spanish, bird songs, and insects chittering. This makes Luna trilingual.

The heart asks to see the ocean. Luna begs her mom to take them to the beach. It takes months of convincing and good grades and helping around the house with chores. Finally, on the first day of summer, they drive to the coast. Luna's mom finds a beach with little traffic in Oceanside. They lug the heart in a wagon. The heart chirps in excitement. It tells Luna, the ocean sounds like a womb. Luna pats the heart and adjusts an umbrella over it to avoid sunburn. Luna, mom, Cheeto in his life vest, and the heart, listen to the ocean for hours in silence. It's what they all agreed on. A day of peace. A day of meditation. Luna journals and doodles into her notebook with a glitter gel pen. Cheeto naps in her lap and dreams about hunting macaques in Sri Lanka. Luna's mom thanks her version of God and reads a romance novel about a shy seamstress who is falling for a woman in NASA who is about to go into space on a secret mission. Luna's mom is impatiently reading for their first kiss and a potential alien invasion. Luna's mom brought ham and cheese sandwiches and mangoes with lime and chili powder for their picnic. Luna chases the ocean back and forth. Cheeto braves the waves and splashes his paws in the water. The heart aches with a new emotion. It's an uncertainty. A feeling of fullness and then nothing. A beat of tenderness and a beat of fear. The family takes a selfie to commemorate their day. The wind intensifies to a point where they can't hear themselves or each other, so they decide to leave. Sand flies into their eyes and into their hair. As they head toward the car, the heart sees the ghost of Ignacio waving to the family. The heart wonders what happened to him but decides not to tell Luna. On the car ride home, Luna and Cheeto nap. The heart watches the forest blur past through the front seat of the car window.

When they get home, Ignacio's ghost is patiently waiting. The heart can sense he's around, but he scatters like some sort of pest when he sees Luna. When the family sleeps, Ignacio comes out and waves at the heart again. The heart shifts the earth underneath, but Ignacio doesn't budge. Ignacio walks to the heart on his own. He touches the heart and asks for a favor. The heart is more curious about how he died. *It was nothing special. An accident!* Ignacio sighs. The heart imagines Ignacio falling into shark infested waters, torn apart like a baby rag doll. *Can you do me a favor?* The heart listens, as Ignacio was its first womb of sorts. *Can I stay with you until I pass on?* The heart is intrigued by this proposition, a potential roommate to help pass the time. The ghost and the unbodied live heart as spectacles together, waiting for death or an earthquake or a flood. The heart agrees to become his new home and Ignacio slips inside through the right atrium and finally falls asleep. He was exhausted from his first day as a ghost. That night, Ignacio dreams of black and white jellyfish swimming in his now decomposing veins.

Years Pass. The heart and Ignacio watch Luna grow up and become a rambunctious teen. They watch her emo phase and her goth phase and her poet phase. They watch as she becomes a confident and brilliant adult. It's beautiful and heart wrenching at the same time. Ignacio remembers why he fell in love with Luna's mom in the first place. He regrets never making more of an effort to meet as a child. There's heartache and longing, but there's the unique privilege of seeing her now, in all of her tenderness. Luna was a gift to the planet. The heart agrees.

Cheeto dies one spring at the age of eighteen. They all mourn together and karaoke Juan Gabriel ballads at the top of their lungs/ventricles because these were Cheeto's favorite songs. He was a romantic and a dreamer. Now, he rests in peace on the fireplace mantle.

When Luna moves out, she leaves the heart a goodbye letter and an offering for her father. She leaves him a jar of sand from Oceanside, where she clearly saw him watching over her for the first time.

MOTHER NATURE

Mami had a bald spot at the crown of her head. Short, rough, black and white hair sprouted up like little seedlings yearning for the sun. She had me scratch her bald spot every night before she fell asleep. The bald spot throbbed, oily and shining under the dim lamp on her pastel pink nightstand. She called it *pipi*. My scratching, not the bald spot. Pipi pronounced like PEE. Pee. Pee. *Mija, dame pipi.* I obeyed and scratched at her bald spot until I heard soft snoring. Her bald spot was a scratch-n-sniff of dirty hair. Hair sitting in the sun with salty sweat slithering down the scalp, down the spine, down behind the knees where capillaries burst into red and purple crooked lines. The bald spot made my fingers smell like nature and pollen and sundrenched hair. Soleado and luminous, I could almost see sunlight project from the curves of my fingerprints.

I thought about scratching deeper into the bald spot, until I saw exposed brain. Could I poke a hole in her head and create a psychic link to her history? Her past. Her childhood. Her reasons for leaving behind an entire country. Her reasons for hiding out when the phone rang. Her reasons for clenching her fists and sighing when she could not take a single step out of the apartment. Mami spoke in short sentences. She was secretive. She was only affectionate on my birthday and on hers. Sometimes, she slept through the morning and into the night, only getting up to go to the bathroom. In her white nightgown, she dragged her feet to the toilet. Her feet scraping at the carpet. I thought of the carpet as a field of wildflowers. My mami, a giant, crushing them under her feet, leaving a trail behind for anyone who wanted to follow her.

I opened the bedroom window for her during thunderstorms and on nights of the full moon. She called it the "fool moon." She said the full moon made people fall in love and love turned people into fools. She told me I was born under desert skies where lost people can see clear clusters of stars in the plum darkness above. Mami told me I was an easy birth. An easy baby. She told me the sun soaked into the roots of her head when I was born. It was too hot to give birth, but she had no choice, and I came out fast.

While Mami slept, I walked around the neighborhood. I explored a few blocks down from where we lived, and scratched at peeling walls and tree trunks. I scratched at sidewalks and asphalt. I scratched so hard, my fingers bled. Even with my bloody fingers, Mami asked me for pipi. What if I peeled under the oily scalp and found polaroids of ancestors? Abuelita in her dark lipstick. Bisabuela and her cockatoos sitting and waiting with a stack of her own family photographs to explore. A continuous chain of photos into our lineage.

In the mornings, I wandered through the apartment complex. I sniffed at the bottom sliver of every door on the first and second floor. I tugged and pushed at doorknobs and sometimes, they let me in. I wandered into kitchens, made myself Kool-Aid, and ate from open bags of chips. I used blue dish soap to wash my face and hands. I traced my fingers over refrigerator magnets and framed photos on the walls. I went through closets and found photo albums. I went through them to see if any of the women in the photos reminded me of Mami before she fell into this cycle. Who was my mami before I was here, watching over her, day after day like a loyal cub?

Once I was done with my home invasions, I wandered behind the apartments and walked along the chain-link fence. I plucked leaves off skinny trees frying in the sun. I scratched the leaves and inhaled their aroma. They smelled like the jungle I ran through over and over in my dreams. A man with crispy skin tapped me on the shoulder. He scratched at his head and dandruff fell in a flurry. I looked up at him with my arms crossed and he shouted at me, "Only the dirt will save us!" I shrugged at him and said, "Probably." Then he ran toward the corner store. I snatched more leaves from the skinny trees and stuffed them into my fanny-pack. My silver fanny-pack was passed down from my tía who also gifted me her old clothes which fit like loose gowns made for an eighties empress with hair like tulle.

Back in the courtyard, I jiggled more doorknobs and one of them let me in. I found scotch tape and stuck the leaves to my arms. They were supposed to be feathers. I stuck leaves to the crown of my head. I found scissors and clipped at my hair. With crooked bangs, I proclaimed, "I am mother nature!" I bolted out of that apartment and ran into mine. Mami was still asleep. Was this her way of getting me used to her death? She wasn't manic anymore, just flesh and bones melting into the bed. I think she was this way for a week or two, the days blurred together. I turned the TV on, it was a Tuesday. Thunderstorms. High Winds. Desert Rain. The pretty pregnant meteorologist pointed at me and said, "I hope you're ready to be mother nature," like she was part of some cheesy informercial. She winked at me and gave me a thumbs up. Mami reached for the remote and waved her hands for me to turn off the TV. I watched as she fell back into her dreams. I kissed her on the forehead and watched her eyelids flutter.

Mugs, glasses, and Big Gulp cups surrounded the bed. I waited until there was no more walking room. I picked up the big gulp cups and stuffed them into a black trash bag until the bag grew into an alien proportion. When I carried the black bag over my shoulder, I thought of myself as a Guatemalan Santa Claus, ready to give free Big Gulp quantities of soda to the kids in the neighborhood. A black kitten rustled in the dumpster. The kitten meowed and leaped from an island of black plastic bags to a pile of white bags thanking the dumpster profusely. *Thank you.Thank you. Thank you.* I reached for the kitten and my hand landed on a scratch-off lottery ticket. I scratched at the skin of the rectangle and the first square was an ocean breeze. I heard the ocean pushing itself toward the shore. Foam appeared on my palms. The second square was a dark forest. The scent of pine rushed into my lungs and soft rain trickled down my head. The third square was a honeysuckle vine. Vines sprouted from the dumpster and followed me back into Mami's room. I could see her shadow sitting straight up on the bed. *Mija, dame pipi.* I obeyed like an easy daughter should. The scabs on my fingertips were starting to peel off. I was shedding. Calloused. Stronger. Faster fingers to ease my mami to sleep, even as vines burst beneath her bed and curl around our bodies like skinny anacondas, mimicking some kind of maternal embrace.

AN ALTAR OF STORIES TO LIMINAL SAINTS

Yvette slicks her graying hair back with green gel and smiles at herself in the mirror. It's three in the morning and she's just had her first cup of coffee. The first cup is always black. She adds creamer to her fourth cup in the afternoon. A sweet treat for a long day. Her shift starts as soon as she hears the doorbell ring. An ethereal ringing and then the light in the apartment turns so bright, it's like staring directly into the sun.

It was alarming at first. Yvette thought the angels were calling to her, to walk into the light, but she was healthy as far as she knew and her Papi always said she was destined for hell.

The very first package was for her. It was a notebook she used to journal in when she was a teenager. In old English lettering, the notebook proclaimed "LESBIANA CHOLA SQUAD." She became close friends with the other three lesbians at school. Chola implied gang, but Yvette wasn't made out for being in a gang, it was more that she was in love with the cholas at her school. She loved their severe eyebrows and Aquanet bangs. She loved how they were down for violence in a heartbeat, out of loyalty to their friends. They were earth angels who never seemed to mind that Yvette and her squad were out without shame. Of course, teenage Yvette was romanticizing them. The cholas were multifaceted. Like the Lesbiana Chola Squad, there was depth beyond the surface of their aesthetics. Yvette thumbed through old journal entries. There were multiple entries with just one word.

Lonely.

Erotic?

FUCK.

There were cringe inducing poems. Love confessions. A lot of love confessions. Yvette blushed. Reading her old passionate scribbles made her sweat. Transported back to teenage angst. Back to the hyper-focused anxiety waves. Yvette got to the last page. There was a phone number written in sharpie.

Call the number.

As a proud old-school mujer and a fan of chisme, Yvette still had a landline.

Yvette dialed the number. There was static on the line. Then a click.

"Mija, I was always proud of you."

It was her Mami on the other line.

"Mami?" Yvette's voiced trembled.

Her mom had been dead for five years at that point.

"I want you to know. I have always been proud of you and sometimes, when I visit you, mija, I leave behind lemon seeds."

Yvette laughed and asked her why.

"Aye, well, the facial expressions you made when you were enojada used to make me laugh. It was a sour face! I always found it endearing, mija. So, lemon seeds! I can do silly shit like that as a ghost."

"Mami, I retired! I started birdwatching and gardening and baking since then. Mami, I miss you."

"I know, mija. I know."

"How's Papi?"

"Stubborn, como siempre. He's always fishing."

"Fishing? Even in death?"

"Even in death."

"Mami, is it really you?"

Yvette felt the lump in her throat and cried, doubting her sanity. How could her Mami be on the other line? Her Mami's voice was crisp and clear and deep. It was so good to hear her voice.

"Of course, it's me, mija. I love you very much, but I have to go. Please be good. Portate bien."

"Mami, can I call you again?"

The dial tone chirped at Yvette. There was someone on the other line.

"Hello?"

A robotic automated message:

"Hello. Yvette. Salazar. Please. Deliver. The. Packages. We send. To you. Until further notice."

"What? Okay?"

The phone went dead.

This morning, Yvette stepped outside and sorted the packages. There were ten packages, every single day. She never shook them or tried to decipher what was inside. She imagined if the automated message came from the office of Jesus himself, it was best not to be curious. Just do the job until the packages stop showing up.

Yvette sat and planned a strategic route on her paper map every morning. She used to be a truck driver and proclaimed herself retired once she saved enough money to pay off Mami and Papi's death debts. Still, she never got tired of cruising around with her music turned up so loud she had no choice but to imagine herself in a music video. There was catharsis in hitting the road with the holy packages. There was no doubt in her mind that the packages changed people's lives. Hers did.

She became a butch fairy of sorts.

Yvette was the proud owner of an emerald Toyota truck with a glittering green cap to cover the bed. It was her favorite self-bought possession. Her truck shimmered in the sun. She named the truck Estrella. Every morning, Yvette greeted Estrella and then said a prayer for both of their safeties.

Yvette wore a variant version of the same thing every day: a long flannel button-up, jeans, and combat boots. She made herself a breakfast burrito with salsa, filled up two water bottles, threw some snacks in her lunch bag and headed out.

Box 1

Andrea got ready for work slowly. A slug's pace. She took her time. She was listening for the front door to confirm he was gone. Andrea washed her face and then moisturized with green tea facial cream. She misted her face with rose water and fanned herself. She took a rose quartz roller and massaged her face. She followed a step-by-step tutorial on how to get the perfect contour, how to make her face shimmer in all the right places. Her lipliner traced perfectly around her lips and she filled the rest in with deep red lipstick to finish up. She used setting spray as the final touch. Her eyeliner was fierce and sharp. Her eyebrows looked like twins. She was fucking proud of how good she looked. She almost forgot to cover the bruises on her wrists. She took cheetah printed bandages to her wrists to cover any evidence of hurt. She carefully slipped into her black turtleneck to cover up the bruising hand marks on her neck. She wriggled into her jeans and put on some cheetah printed flats. From the bathroom, she heard the front door slam shut. Andrea stepped out of the bathroom quietly and when she walked into the living room, he was waiting for her. He asked her what took her so goddamn long. He asked her why she wasn't speaking to him. Why was she hiding from him? Andrea blurted out that she was tired and didn't want to argue anymore. He stomped into the kitchen, ran his hands under hot water, walked back to the living room, shoved Andrea against a wall, took both his wet hands to her face, and pressed so hard she thought her eyeballs would burst out. He smudged her makeup onto her black turtleneck, picked her up by the hair, and dragged her into the kitchen where he pinned her to the floor. He tore open a package of sanitizing wipes and he scraped at her face with them. Andrea cried as he finally stopped, got up, and smiled. He screamed fuck you fuck you fuck you as he walked out the front door, letting it slam behind him. Andrea took in a deep breath and sobbed into her hands. She crawled to the door and watched him drive away. She noticed a small box on the porch. She went out to grab the box and could hear it thumping. She opened the box and a human heart with a white ribbon tied around it continued to thump. A note from sender stated *BOIL ME. BURY ME IN LOCUST GROVE CEMETERY.* Andrea looked up *Human Heart Pranks* online to see if this was some sort of viral trick. She searched for answers on her phone and then said fuck it. If she was going to die at the hands of a stupid fucking animal she might as well just take this note at its word. She untied the white ribbon and dunked the heart into boiling water. The heart continued to thump and left behind a sweet aroma, like lavender. The heart turned deep purple as it boiled and continued to thump. She placed it back into the box. She changed into her favorite dress. It was hidden in a secret compartment which she added into the closet. She washed her face and then wiped it clean. She screamed into the mirror. She stepped out without locking the door behind her. She got into her car and took three deep breaths to shake out the nerves in her hands. She took the box with her newly gifted heart and she placed the seatbelt around it. She patted the box and input Locust Grove Cemetery into her GPS. It would take thirty minutes to get there. Andrea had a playlist for days she was most scared. They were songs that she used to karaoke in high school and songs her mom used to play on Sunday mornings to wake her up to clean. She looked ahead and started to drive. As Andrea got to the last stop light before her final destination, she looked to her right and watched as the driver in a bright green truck belted out the ballad that was booming from their speakers. Andrea continued her journey and parked at the cemetery entrance. She wasn't sure where to bury the heart that thumped in the seat next to her. She opened the box again and the note stated *BURY ME under an OAK TREE.* There was only one oak tree she could see. Easy enough. Andrea ran into the cemetery with the heart in her purse. She ran to the oak tree and apologized to it for what she was about to do. With her stubby fingernails, she dug into the earth. She placed the heart into the hole and stacked fresh dirt on the organ.

She hid the burial site under leaves she pulled from the oak tree. The heart continued to thump and Andrea could feel the ground beneath her feet move like a heartbeat. She drove back to the apartment and packed all of her underwear and socks. She packed some clothes and all of her makeup. She started driving to Texas. She chose Texas because she missed good Mexican food and nosy neighbors.

Her ex was pronounced dead that same day.

He died from heart complications.

Box 2

Nayeli had the same dream again. She saw herself lined up as multiple versions of herself. As a baby all the way to forty-two. Her dog, Mochi, came along with each version, and each version of Nayeli had a treat for Mochi. Nayeli woke up to an empty bedroom. Mochi was dead. He was taken by coyotes on the summer night he snuck out of the house. Nayeli still doesn't know how. Mochi was sweet, but never clever. How did he manage to escape? Nayeli was out dancing with friends. She came home to a wide-open door and no Mochi.

The doorbell rang and Nayeli looked through the peephole. She saw someone in flannel dropping off a box on the porch. Nayeli waited for them to leave and she slipped out quickly to grab the box. Inside of the box was a bell. A note inside the box stated *RING MY BELL*. Nayeli shook the bell back and forth. She put the bell next to a photo of Mochi.

Nayeli went to work, went about her typical day. When she got home, Mochi's ghost was waiting for her. Nayeli shook her head, squeezed her eyes shut until she saw purple stars, opened them again, and Mochi was still there with his tongue out, patiently waiting for her to pet him. All Nayeli could think was, what kinds of treats can a ghost dog eat?

<u>Box 3</u>

Jaime is on vacation. The package on his porch is torn open by a racoon. The racoon finds a pomegranate inside the box. The note in the box is blank because the racoon can't read. The racoon takes the pomegranate to a vacant house where it will spend the night. The racoon embraces the pomegranate and dreams about swimming in a pond filled with trash. The trash is delicious and the pomegranate sits on the shore of the pond glowing green. The racoon eats all of the garbage and wakes up in a good mood.

Box 4

Sarita pours old coffee into a cup and sips it while she watches her morning cartoons. Her mommy has left her alone again. No note this time. She hasn't called her and it's almost been a week. Sarita finishes her coffee and gets into her school uniform. She hasn't been able to wash it since her mommy left so she sprays her clothes with air freshener. She makes sure to put on deodorant. Her armpits stink, or this is what her classmate, Rene, tells her. She's out of toothpaste, so she brushes her teeth with hot water. She sucks on a cough drop to fake the feeling of fresh breath. She brushes her long hair and swirls it into a large bun on her head. She knocks on her mommy's door and says bye. It's for comfort. Sarita knows there's nothing on the other side. As Sarita steps out, a package sits on the porch. Sarita shakes the box. She takes it with her into the apartment courtyard. She can't help but open it. Inside, a tiny doll with long brown hair and big brown eyes stares at her. The note inside states *PLAY WITH ME*. Sarita names the doll Eva. Eva was born in the Redwood Forest. Eva is a fairy princess. Eva makes magical portals with rocks. She creates an enchanted circle to step into, gets in, and then she's transported. Sarita makes a rock circle in the center of the courtyard. She closes her eyes and then steps inside. Sarita is in the Redwood Forest with Eva. Eva and Sarita run around like beautiful wild things. They howl at each other, they laugh like little hyenas, they swim in the river water, climb up the trees, higher and higher until they can touch the clouds. Sarita looks at Eva and asks her if they could be like this forever. Eva nods and launches herself off the top of the tree. Sarita looks at the moon and takes in the fragrance of the forest. Sarita smells like the earth. Sarita launches herself with her face toward the sky. The fall is fast, her body breaks twigs in half, she can hear her heartbeat rapid and roaring, she can see her mommy's face worried about her, finally, really worried about her. Or would she be relieved? Sarita falls into the forest floor, where she can see rabbit families huddled in soft lumps. She wants to hold them. She wants warmth. Sarita wants someone to hold her.

Box 5

Lupe needs a clove of garlic so her fideo will taste right. She's stuck at home because her son wanted to borrow the car. He got into a fender bender and his car is in the shop. Or so he says. Her son is mysterious in ways that make no sense. Why doesn't he tell her where he works? Why doesn't he go to church? Why is he always texting on his phone? WHO is he texting? Anyway, Lupe peeks outside and sees Rodrigo tending to his rock garden and succulents. He's shirtless. Lupe finds his belly endearing and she can't believe he still shows off his body, at his age. She doesn't mind, but still, at his age. She closes the blinds fast, but something in her wants to get caught. Rodrigo is married, well, his wife is dead, he's a widower. Lupe has a feeling that his wife is still there, in another form, of course. Lupe is startled by the doorbell. A green truck drives away. A package sits next to her collection of angel statues. She takes the package inside and opens it. A head of garlic sits in the box. The note inside states *FOR THE SOUP*!! Lupe wonders if Rodrigo sent this to her.

At her age, she could still look for love. Maybe. She just doesn't want drama from afterlife wives. Lupe examines the head of garlic, she takes a clove, minces it and adds it to her fideo. Once the soup is done, Lupe pours herself a bowl, adds lime, and waits for it to cool off. As she slurps from her spoon, the tumor in her head shrinks to the size of a pea. As she finishes her bowl, the tumor disappears. Lupe is hoping her son will come home soon. She has her list of questions. First, she will ask if he wants some soup and then she will ask about his day and she will watch his eyes for his lies. She knows she will always love him all the same. Lupe sits in silence and then decides she needs some sun. She puts on red lipstick and heads out the front door. She walks across the street to see if Rodrigo will answer his door. She wants to talk to him about his kids and hers. Remember when their eyes were so bright, it made your chest ache? She wants to talk to him about his day. She wants a little drama in her life. Lupe hopes the ghost of his wife is there.

Box 6

Ana's Mami tugs at her hair to put it up in a high bun. She kisses her forehead and picks lint off of her uniform sweater. It's Ana's day for show and tell. She has three things in mind.

(1.) A rock she found by a tidepool where purple and orange fat starfish nestled on the rocks. Sometimes, the rock rolls around in her room on its own. Ana doesn't know who plays with the rock at night. She hides under her blanket and doesn't dare look under the bed. So, the rock.

(2.) Then, there's her favorite leaf. Her Mami and Papi took her to the forest where she watched banana slugs slither in wet leaves. She took the biggest yellow leaf she could find and saved it in her backpack. She took it home with her and now it sits beautiful and crinkled behind a frame that her Mami made her. So, the leaf.

(3.) Then, there's the package that she found early in the morning. It sat on the front porch. When Ana looked down from her window, a doe came to nose at it and bunnies hopped on the porch to sniff at it. Ana snuck downstairs and opened the front door to grab the package. She took it upstairs and when she opened the box, rays of sunlight warmed her face. The note in the box states *FOR SHOW AND TELL*.

Ana decides to take the package to school. She's unsure on how to present it to the class, it's just an unlabeled box. She can make it a game. Ask the class what they think is inside of the box.

In front of the class, Ana says she's going to perform a magic trick. She asks the class to sit in a circle around her and close their eyes. She opens the box and the light is so bright, her eyes water. She closes her eyes and sees her last birthday party. Everything was pastel purple and her Mami let her wear mascara. Her Papi surprised her. He was supposed to be at some boring conference overseas. They ate confetti cake and danced all night. She was so happy in this moment.

Leonel sees himself painting on a canvas with his big brother, Juan. Leonel paints spirals and multicolored spiderwebs. Juan paints a realistic portrait of their Pomeranian, El Tigre. When the portrait is finished, they give it to their mom and she's surprised and delighted. That night, they eat pizza and watch anime together until they can no longer stay awake.

Janine sees herself playing on the beach. Hundreds of tourists gathered by the shore because a dolphin pod was leaping and playing in the distance. Her mom and dad are both there. They shared a pair of binoculars to get a closer look at the dolphins. Her mom and dad also shared chicharrónes de harina with

Valentina hot sauce as they cheered on Janine who was doing cartwheels to impress the dolphins. This was a day where they didn't fight. Janine wasn't scared of her dad and they had such a good day, it ended with ice cream.

The teacher sees herself as a newborn. Being swaddled and held. She can feel the warmth of her mother singing her to sleep. The sensation is overwhelming. She stifles her tears of joy in this moment.

The fly in the room sees itself as a firefly. The firefly is one of hundreds, floating above swampland where manatees sleep and unexplainable creatures lurk.

When the class opens their eyes, they applaud the magic trick. Ana is confused but elated. She puts the box inside her cubby and the class spends the rest of the day talking about what they saw.

Box 7

Denise wakes up on the bathroom floor. Flashes of her night blur together. She was hiding again. The love of her life slipped a note under the bathroom door. An apology note for the night before. Denise looks into the mirror and pokes at her fat lip. Her hair is a mess. Her hair is short now. The man she loves decided in a rage that Denise should be bald. He also slipped sleeping pills into Denise's drinks because she threatened to go out with her friends that night. Denise had to drag herself to the bathroom and lock herself in. She splashes her face with water and takes in a deep breath. She calls her sister to cancel her plans. She can't come visit anymore. She refuses to explain herself. *Tell the babies I love them.* She steps out of the bathroom and sits on the couch next to her love as he sleeps. A package outside thumps and thumps waiting for someone to open it.

Box 8

Jude finds a package on the front porch. He opens it and a bear figurine sits in the box. The note inside states *PLAY WITH ME*. Jude takes the bear into his room and the figurine bear comes alive. The bear yawns and stands on its hind legs. It climbs up the bunk bed and nestles into the blankets. Jude goes up the ladder to look for the bear. The bear runs at Jude. Jude opens his small hands to the bear, and it settles into his cupped palms. Jude wants to show his mom and dad and big brother. They recently lost their Bichon Frise named Luc. Luc ran away. The boys say that the forest fairies took Luc. When Jude brings the bear with him to dinner, he lets it loose on the table. The bear goes for the mashed potatoes and Jude's mom shrieks. *Is it a mouse?* She looks closer and sees it's a miniaturized grizzly bear. *Can I please keep it?* Big brother votes yes. Mom and Dad are unsettled by the small guy. Where did he come from? But they both agree that the grizzly can stay downstairs. That night, the grizzly sneaks upstairs and cuddles Jude. Jude whispers fairy tales and scary stories to the bear. When the grizzly farts like a trumpet, the boys roar in laughter. Mom and Dad ask each other if they made the right choice. The bear would say yes. Jude and big brother would say yes. Mom, Dad, grizzly, Jude, and big brother dream about the redwood giants that night.

Box 9

Linda shuffles around her studio apartment waiting for something in her life to shift. Should she just quit her job? Should she move to the wilderness? Linda suffers from a broken heart, or at least that's what she says. She doesn't miss her ex as much as she misses the cat, Lady Gaga. Lady Gaga and Linda had a soul connection. Her pendeja ex stole Lady Gaga in the break-up. She threatened to get litigious if Linda wanted to fight for custody. The relationship ended on boring terms. The threat of legal action was the most action they both got out of the relationship. They got tired of the other and that was that. Now, Linda has an excuse to play *Sea Change* on repeat and weep for the cat. The doorbell rings. Linda slips outside in her lavender robe and slippers. She shouts THANK YOU! to the delivery person who is getting into a lime green truck that glistens in the sun. Linda's hair has been in a messy bun for the last three days. She called in sick, she needed to mourn. She picks up the package and shakes it. It sounds like bells. Linda opens the box.

The note inside states *FOLLOW ME*. One small orb of light floats out of the box. Linda tries to touch it and it goes through the front door. She follows the orb into oncoming traffic. People honk. Linda doesn't hear them. The orb leads Linda into the playground of her old elementary school. Children squeal and shriek in giddiness while playing freeze tag. Linda squints and sees herself as a child. She sees Arturo and Yolanda as kids. She hasn't seen these friends in over twenty years. Little Linda tags Arturo and yells Freeze! The orb floats around them, teasing them as they reach for it. Then it disappears. The kid versions of her past stare at Linda and then simultaneously point into the woods. When Linda steps into the forest, thousands of orbs surround her. When she reaches to touch them, they burst like soap bubbles. More orbs attach themselves to her until her robe is full and her hair is full and her face is full. The orbs pick her up. They lift her past the trees and the skyscrapers of downtown. They lift her up, up, up. Linda wants them to drop her, only because she's always wanted to skydive.

Box 10

Death is looking for her next client, but her internal GPS isn't working. She's at the top of a hill. Pine fills the air. She knows what the client looks like, she has her folder in hand, with all her major life events listed, one by one, not for judgement, but just in case the client has any questions. Questions like, whatever happened to my best friend in first grade? Answer: [Confidential] Is fate real? Answer: [Redacted]. Is there a heaven and hell? Answer: [Redacted]. She's running late, which technically, is never supposed to happen, but THE SYSTEM is down. No one at HQ will give any further details which means this has probably never happened before. Death runs into Death 8.642 and they nod heads at each other. Death 8.642 is searching for a body that is now buried under moss. Death watches Yvette Salazar drop off a package on the porch of a quaint yellow house. Julieta Castillo opens the door and shakes the box. A small cry of a baby startles her. Death shakes off her nerves and touches up her dark violet lipstick. She places her veil over her face and heads toward Julieta's house. She's found her client.

Yvette watches her rearview mirror. A woman in a black jumpsuit and black veil waves at her. Yvette waves back and drives away. She has chills up her neck and down her spine. When Yvette gets home, she tries to call her Mami again. An answer.

"Mami? Is this you?"

"Mija! Please listen. Go to THE GARDEN. It's a bar."

Of course, Yvette had gone to THE GARDEN before.

"Why?"

"You're going to meet the love of your life."

"Mami, you know I'm okay being alone."

"I know. But please, give this a chance."

Yvette sucks in her teeth and says "Okay. I'll do it."

"Love you, mija."

"Love you, Mami."

Yvette takes a shower, washes her face, brushes her teeth. She puts on red and black flannel with black jeans. She slicks back her short hair. She tells herself she's doing this for Mami. When she gets to the bar, there are only three people there. One person at the bar, and two cholas playing pool. Yvette sits at the bar. She nods at the woman at the end of the bar. The woman gives Yvette a warm smile. An, *I don't mind if you come over and talk to me*, smile.

Her Mami was right. It's a whirlwind romance. It's a romantic comedy. Sometimes a dramedy. One time, it was almost a haunted house romance but they decided not to move into that house. Yvette and Regina get married. Yvette and Regina connect in a way that could only be remade into a movie as a moody lesbian drama where one of them paints the other and then they meet life after life as different versions of artist and muse.

The packages stop showing up. Mami stops answering the phone. Yvette thinks of all the magic surrounding her all those years, the miracles, the liminal saints who showed up and led her to Regina. Yvette kisses Regina on the forehead and then her lips, they lean into each other as they watch their nightly telenovelas where the main characters are guaranteed to find love and happiness.

POSTPARTUM IS FOREVER

The Botánica Flashback

The Curandero says he can raise my chances of getting pregnant from forty percent to seventy percent. His hands are adorned with gold rings and tattoos. His eyes are big and brown and honest. He points at my crotch and tells me he sees a dark triangular shadow around my uterus. A force of evil. We're in the back of the Botánica and the room smells like Florida water, incense, and melted wax. A gigantic Saint Michael portrait hangs on the wall in a gaudy gold frame along with what I assume are Curandero certificates of credentials. A robust and intimidating muscular statue of Archangel Michael watches from the corner. His sword shines above his head and Satan looks annoyed that he's being stepped on. I make direct eye contact with the Curandero. I tell him in broken Spanish that I could guess why the shadows lurk around my, *como se dice*, vagina. My guess is years of bodily trauma. I point between my legs and tell him there's been a lot of bad news in there, but he shakes his head NO.

It's not that I wanted to get pregnant. I never thought about bringing someone earthside before. The thought of a creature swimming inside my belly made me feel vulnerable in the worst way. It made me nauseous. It made my belly itchy. My body, making lungs, creating a placenta, a vibrating heart, and passing down the depth of ancestral love, but also the traumatizing bullshit. Bringing something to life means it eventually has to die. I didn't say this to the Curandero. I let him rub the egg I handpicked from the baby blue carton on my stomach and my chest. I closed my eyes and saw myself in a pastel pink room with fleshy walls, soft, and dripping iridescent liquid onto my hand. I licked at my palms and the walls quivered and vibrated. Moans came from under my feet. I trembled, my body pulsating into a deep trance. My body twitched and my belly buzzed with warmth. I opened my eyes and I was back in the Botánica. The Curandero kept praying over me and I don't remember getting on my knees, but I was kneeled in front of him, and the wall filled with crosses, marigolds, and a painting of the Mexican version of Jesus with a six-pack, blue eyes, and a head dripping with glittering blood. Sweat dribbled down my temples. My clothes stuck to me from my fever visions. I heaved in and out. My heartbeat was thunderous. I was sobbing. I was confused. I was euphoric.

The Curandero claimed he saw my baby on the other side as he performed the cleansing. A healthy baby boy with the attitude of a bull. My love for him would be an inescapable and beautiful bond. He put his right hand on my forehead and then over my heart. I fainted in slow motion and he placed me on a comforter with a La Virgen de Guadalupe design, doting on me as I thrashed around on her. You have to understand, this isn't how my cleansings usually went. I would go in, feel some tingling at the tips of my fingers and toes, but that was it. With this vaginal aura cleansing, I felt like those gyrating Evangelical sweaty people on TV. Something overtook me. The Curandero played along, and we both got so into it, I really fainted, and he really saw something on the other side, I just don't know if it was my son.

In the backroom of the Botánica, I napped in a corner as other clients came in. No one seemed to mind. Some of them gave me small tokens. Flower petals. Coins. Smooth rounded rocks from their pockets. I had vivid all-consuming dreams. First, in a room with white glossy walls, bright lights surrounding me as I gave birth to a gigantic baby with a full set of teeth. I was tied down to the bed with white leather straps. My hospital gown was ripped apart and bloody. A glowing faceless entity untied me from the bed. The baby looked up at me and smiled with all its teeth and I could not bring myself to hold him. In another dream, I was on the beach, my pregnant belly soaking in the sun, and exquisite green quetzals with shining ruby bellies flew past me. My eyes followed as they flew into the cloud forest. I tried to trail them, but the forest was dense and thick with fog. Eyes watched me from the trees. I looked down at my belly and could see my son kicking hard. I touched the outdent of his foot. I looked down at my palms and eyes blinked at me from the center of each palm. I rubbed my belly and my palms could see inside. I was going to give birth to a quetzal. In the third dream, I met myself as a child. She wore our favorite floral printed dress with a side ponytail in a red scrunchie. Her wrists were adorned in neon beaded bracelets. Her sneakers were bright white and her socks had tiny ladybugs on them. She was excited to meet me. She shook my hand and smiled with her cute little front gap. Curly baby hairs stuck out of the front of her head as though they were impala horns. She skipped as she led me to a small cave where she buried flash cards of her favorite words she just learned in English. Rompe Cabezas: Puzzles. Respirar: Breathe. Arcoíris: Rainbow. She looked up at me and I wanted to turn away so she couldn't see what would hide behind her eyes in a few years. She pointed up at the sky and there were three suns. Orange. Yellow. Purple. The clouds were swirls. The air smelled like roses and burning wood. Albino crows yelled and chased each other. I wanted to thank her for meeting with me. As I looked down at her, her eyes were gone. Blood lined her small face. I tried to hold her, but she disappeared into ash.

A Memory

When I was five, my mom slapped me across the face because I walked in on her hiding bricks of marijuana in her bedroom closet. It was the early nineties and she met a man who promised her a new kind of life if she worked for him. My tía Alicia believed the same thing and she ended up in a Zacatecas prison. My tía got caught smuggling drugs minutes before she was about to cross the Mexican border into Texas. Mom grabbed me by the chin and told me to stay out of her room and to mind my business when strangers came through the apartment, especially Uncle Nestor. Nestor was a pervert. He was rude and told nasty jokes. He pinched my ass at any chance he got. He blew kisses at me when no one was looking. I flipped him off when no one was looking. My cheek throbbed. I closed my eyes and took in a deep breath. I was furious. I wished I could slap my mom back until her lips split open.

You know how I knew I was pregnant with you? On the first day of spring, seven ladybugs landed on my belly. There were huge swarms of them all over the city that year. If you opened your mouth to yawn, a little ladybug could fly down your throat and get lost in your gut, but seven meant new life. It meant you found me in this new life.

Then, she explained that tía Alicia was a murderer in her prior life, but the worst kind. She was a serial killer. She didn't want to terrify me with the details. Tía Alicia was repaying her debts in this life. I remember a long bus ride and the cobblestone roads on the way to the prison. It wasn't a family visit, it was a business meeting. My mom showed up to inform my tía of the financial debts she would owe after she was released. My tía spit on mom and mom brushed it off saying it might take my tía two more lives before that man in her soul can repent for what he did. I wondered if this was Nestor's first life. He was a bad man. He didn't even try to disguise it. He was the man who taught me that sometimes my soul and my body could detach. For survival.

My Son Introduces Himself

It was after work. It was evening and the pink sky was fading. My mind was preoccupied with a man in the office. He looked like a human version of a pug and he put his hands on me. He grabbed me by the neck and squeezed until I started to panic, then he called it a joke. This wasn't the first time he touched me. I could tell he was testing his boundaries. Pushing, little by little. I wanted to smother the pug man. I wanted to rip out his tongue and feed it to the hawks. If he dropped dead, I would celebrate.

After washing frustration tears off my face, I looked into the mirror of my tiny bathroom, and I heard a whisper in my right ear. The air was warm.

I'm ready.

I'm ready to be born.

I want to be born.

It didn't scare me. I just knew it was the truth.

There's a superstition that says if someone is calling your name as you're falling asleep, not to follow the voice because it's a trick. An entity is trying to gain your trust and then take advantage of you. If it's a Catholic, they'll say it's a demon. If it's a witch, she'll say it's an enemy. I don't know what the advantage is, maybe giving you a night terror so intense you vomit or maybe a tall shadow figure to choke you as you writhe in bed, helpless and numb. My method of protection is to acknowledge the voice and then curse at it. I shout a stream of consciousness string of curse words, tell it I am not afraid, and end the conversation by telling it to fuck off.

This voice was different.

This voice knew my name and then told me theirs.

A Burrowing Owl Shows Up

Being pregnant made me morbid. I wanted to know all the ways I could die. I consumed as many true crime stories as possible. I read the tabloids, listened to podcasts, watched documentaries. It all made me sick to my stomach, but I thought of it as building an armor. A thicker skin for understanding how unfair the world can be to a child. These stories made me see the world in a color palette of grays and burnt yellow. Every single day, real people face this despair. Some of them disappear without a trace. The existential dread made me see faces out of the corner of my eye, but I needed to know what kind of sadistic people were out there. How could someone rip another person limb from limb and then bury them in their backyard? How could someone hide a body in a barrel? How could someone keep another human locked in a small coffin under their bed? How could they do these things and move on with their days, with their lives? Who are these people that lurk in the shadows? It's rarely strangers. Statistically, pregnancy upped my chances of death. I was a waddling vulnerable member of society, a sciatic nerve away from collapsing. Who was most likely to murder me? Always the partner. Whether, asphyxiation, drowning, a bullet, he would be the first person suspected. That sits in the back of my mind. My partner could kill me if he wanted. Who was most likely to get blamed if anything goes wrong with the baby? Always the mother. Mommy. Mami. Mom. Mama.

My mom says she saw the aftermath of a murder while she was pregnant with me. It was coincidental. A synchronicity of bad luck. She was craving chips with hot sauce and lime. A burrowing owl swooped through the automatic doors and hopped at her swollen feet as she entered the grocery store. While feeling for smooth limes, an unassuming man in khakis and a white button up shirt waited at the register. The cashier waved to him as he waited for her to finish ringing up the person ahead of him, her smile faded as the man got closer. The little owl hopped at my mom's feet and then flew toward the back of the store. She decided to follow the owl. As my mom trailed behind the owl, the man in khakis held a pistol to the head of the cashier and pulled the trigger. She fell forward, onto the conveyor belt, and her blood slowly poured down to the scuffed-up tile floor. People screamed and scattered in panic. My mom was in the backroom of the store where she frantically found an exit. She was so shocked and afraid, she climbed up a ladder stacked against the back side of the grocery store and hid behind the ledge of the roof. She peeked over and watched as the khaki man walked out of the store slowly. He walked to the payphone booth, made a call, then shot himself. My mom held her face in her hands and screamed. She watched as the little owl hopped around the booth.

It was a father and daughter. The khaki man will come back as a garden snake in his next life and then a cricket in the next. She told me the cashier's mother kept some of her daughter's teeth, hair and her ashes in a locket as an offering she planned on leaving to a generous god. Her daughter's name was Genesis.

Genesis will come back as a human again. A child destined for love from a happy family. Genesis will grow old and watch as her grandchildren bloom into kind people.

Labor

I had to be induced because my obstetrician was concerned that I had too much fluid in my womb. It was poly-something. I never looked up the rest of the word. Going online is a curse when you're pregnant. The first nurse was nice enough, but she was new. Her hands trembled as she searched for a vein in my wrist. She missed at her first go and a line of blood trickled down my forearm. Induction meant Cytotec. It had to be inserted vaginally. I was on bedrest from thirteen weeks on. This meant no sex, no orgasms, no penetration. Nice new nurse had large hands. Even with the lubricant on her blue gloved hand, it was excruciating to have her fingers inside me. She couldn't get the pill to stick the first time. She had to try again. She shoved what felt like her entire hand into me and I couldn't help but let out a yelp. I held my partner's hand and squeezed to give him an indication of the pain that jolted up my body. As calmly as I could, I took in a deep breath, and I told myself I was going to be okay.

I was about to be in labor for thirty-two hours.

I had a suspicion that my birthing experience would be difficult. Call it intuition or a curse. I was meant to be in the stiff and sterile hospital room. A little bloated science experiment. It made sense for my body story. Contractions feel like period cramps with the volume turned up so high, you feel like you could throw up, but you don't or can't because the next wave of pain is going to make you forget to breathe. Breathing. You have to think about breathing more than ever because this is the key to easing a baby out. Or that's what I read, but it wasn't true for me. I was never one with the pregnancy cosmos. I read plenty of pregnancy blogs with women who were in their element. They loved being pregnant and more than anything, they were ready to give birth. I was not exhilarated to tear myself apart. I was not ready for the inevitability that is birth. I was scared. I wasn't ready, but I had no choice.

After eight hours of contractions, I wanted my body to do what it was supposed to. I wasn't dilating. Nothing was happening except for the induced contractions. There was no indication that I had made any progress at all. I was frustrated and in pain. So, I asked for epidural. I waited for the anesthesiologist as the nurse explained that I had to sit very still so the needle would go smoothly into my lower back. I nodded and breathed through more contractions. Because I would be numb from the waist down, the nurses would have to help me move and I would need a catheter. I nodded and waited. As the needle pricked my back, I felt a sense of relief and once I was numb, I was euphoric for a couple of hours.

My mom takes it upon herself to show up at the birth of each grandchild. I think it was around 12 hours into my labor that she showed up uninvited. I was numb from the waist down; my pain was gone, so I didn't mind her there on the sidelines. My relationship with my mom is complicated and distorted. It's hard to explain if you weren't there. We love each other, but most days, we cannot stand each other. I finally dilated to two centimeters, and then to three centimeters. At this point, my doctor recommended for my water to be broken. With my legs open and lifted in stirrups, she manually broke my water. I imagined myself as a giant water balloon. Through my numbness, I could tell that liquid was spilling on the bed, it was very warm, it was abundant. I thought of myself as a blue whale landing on a shore and blowing out my womb water.

24 Hours

My mom says I was born to spite someone from my most recent past life. I was pregnant in that life. I used to live somewhere with a lot of snow. Mountains lined the skyline. Two giant statues stood at the edge of the town. I died buried under snow. I died before giving birth. My old bones are still out there, so are my sons'. This is what she tells me as the epidural starts to wear off and my back feels like it is being ripped open. I want to pull out her hair. I want to shove her into mud. I want to tell her to fuck off. My partner pulls her away from me and asks her to please leave the room.

I let out helpless whimper after whimper. It's automatic. I am no longer in control of how I manage the pain. It is the entirety of my body. I don't want to be in it anymore. The nurse does not believe me when I tell her I can no longer stand the pain. I grab the vomit bags next to me and throw up Jell-O and broth. It has been over twenty-four hours and I want to give up. I sob into my hands and ask the nurse to please help me with the pain. From outside my room, my mom overhears the commotion, so she takes matters into her own hands. She goes to the lead nurse and tattles on apathetic nurse. The lead nurse comes in to check on me, different nurses come in to check on me. I get more epidural. I go numb again from the waist down.

The first time I saw my son, he was a lone bat. He was a spastic little Mexican free-tailed bat in the desert sky. He jolted in a zig zag and then disappeared. The second time I saw him, he was a buckeye butterfly. He landed on my shoes and in my hair over and over. He followed me and my partner and fluttered around us while we sat and birdwatched at the park across the street from our apartment. This is the third time I have caught a glimpse of him. The nurses prop a mirror in front of me so I can observe what is happening. I watch as his head barely pokes out of me and then slides back in. Over and over. His hair is much lighter than mine, but I can tell he is just as stubborn. I am in extreme exhaustion. I pass out between each push. My eyes roll back as though I am under a spell. The nurse continues to yell

PUSH! I wake up over and over to push and then promptly pass out.

I see bats hanging from the hospital ceiling. Scattering around and then huddling together into one of the corners. I see a small child waving at me with an eye in their palm. I smile at the child and the child playfully sticks their tongue out at me. I see curved galaxies swirling in the walls of the room. Buckeye butterflies swarm my body.

Then, there he is.

As soon as my son is placed on my chest, he coos and grunts. As he lets out his first earthside cries, I feel relief. Then, what I imagine giving birth to the head of a jellyfish feels like, the placenta that nourished him slides out and the doctor plops it into a blue bucket next to the bed. I rock my son gently as the doctor sews me up. He is six pounds, one ounce. He is pink and wrinkled perfection. As I look into his eyes, I know I would do anything for him. I would come back life after life after life just to hear his raspy cries.

GENETIC SHADOWS OF A CHOLA

I found an abandoned eyebrow pencil on Mami's bathroom floor. The pencil was shorter than my pinkie, but the brown tip of the pencil had some life in it. The cap and the exterior of the pencil were cherry red. It felt like I'd found a piece of jewelry. A piece of art. I traced the outer lines of my lips then puckered at the mirror. I used to kiss wet dirt as it rained. I claimed it was because I could taste who the clouds were mourning but, it was for vanity. It was for glamour. I wanted the mud to look like lipstick. I wanted to be a painted diva.

I found a piece of my Mami as I looked into the mirror and into my dark eyes. Mami was a teenage chola in the seventies. I found this out while she was at one of her jobs. She worked at three of the marts with a letter in front of their names. K-mart, S-mart, T-mart, I can't remember which ones. I knew Mami hid her stamp collection and photographs behind the towels in the linen closet. I committed federal crimes for those stamps. She used to send me off so I could go through the mailboxes in neighborhoods with pretty rows of houses. The houses were identical, right down to their manicured lawns and screaming sun decoration that each house hung by their front doors.

"Mija, it's only the stamps. It's not like you're opening their mail to be a chismosa. It's not like you're stealing their money."

I took an envelope opener and slid it through so no damage occurred to the papers inside, I cut the stamped corners off with haircutting scissors. I was fast. I could collect fifty new stamps in under an hour. As a symbol of rebellion, Mami burned the stamps of American flags and dusted their ashes into the wind. She told me this was as political as she could get until she passed her citizenship test.

Red towels and white tiger cobijas were stacked neatly inside the linen closet. I grabbed each piece one by one, stacked them on the floor until there was space for me to grab the photo satchel. I lugged the brown satchel into the hallway and imagined what it was like to be in each one as I shuffled through them.

In her chola days, Mami wore her bangs close to the sky. Her curls were voluminous and bloomed over her shoulders. Her lips had a dark brown line around them and her eyebrows looked furious, like cartoon boomerangs. She looked like a Mexican Dolly Parton, except with plaid and Dickies. In my favorite chola photo of her, she's in a white tank top and deep blue jeans with white flowers stitched to the flares of the legs. She's standing proudly in front of a rose garden. I could smell the roses and the dirt as I looked into her eyes in that photo. On the back, she wrote: *Dark Eyes. Lost Soul. Beautiful Thorns.*

With the brown lines around my lips, I looked so much like her at that moment. I shouted brave things, things like "Soy una chingona!" and "Te mato con mis ojos!" because those were the phrases I heard Mami shout at herself when she thought I wasn't listening. I got to know pieces of her through photographs while she worked her multiple shifts, then came home to nap during the day. She used to bring me holographic stickers, butterfly clips, and jelly shoes in glittering variations of colors. I made sure to adorn myself with her gifts. It was a reciprocal cycle of her showing me she loved me and me showing her I loved her in spite of being gone most days.

Through her photographs, I found out about her past marriage. She was covered in white lace with her arms wrapped around a man I never knew. Her smile was so bright and overwhelming. Looking at it felt holy. It was the only thing I could focus on in the photo. She loved taking pictures of birds. Birds in intricate cages. Birds the color of sweet mangoes and bitter limes. Birds forming geometry in the sky. Someone took a photo of Mami in front of El Castillo in Chichen Itzá. On the back she wrote: *Lineage, sacrifice, and listening to the echoes of my ancestors, 1987.*

In photos where white hair sprinkled her head, Mami never smiled. She started graying at thirty years old. In their gray-haired days, my abuela and my great-grandmami didn't smile in photos either. I followed their path. I had no white strands of hair on my head, but I felt kinship to old souls. I never smiled in my school pictures or in photos of my birthday parties. I was stubborn. In my birthday hat and confetti covered living room, I gave a serious face to the camera. Even with school picture re-dos, I refused to smile.

Each time I was done with my diva act, I wiped the chola art off of my lips and hid the short pencil in my room. I kept it hidden inside of a bright yellow sock. I filled that with glitter and then hid the sock in the belly of a stuffed elephant. It was a love spell to myself.

We moved out of those apartments and moved into a house after Mami met a woman who was in the Navy. She was pale with dark blond hair and spoke German in her sleep. She gave me a digital watch, a calculator, and an encyclopedia set from the 1960's when we first met. She claimed these items would help me take over the world. I told her I was going to take over the world with a camera. I watched as she and Mami became closer and then eventually fell into the kind of love where corny jokes were gold and family nights meant the three of us plus her two polite daughters.

After we moved out of the apartments, I lost the eyebrow pencil and Mami lost her bags of photos. I imagined the photos scattered in the sky and landing into backyards and bird baths. I imagined some of them disappearing into golden dusts and others into pink star matter.

For my tenth birthday, I asked for a disposable camera. I took photos of Mami while she cooked. I caught the smoke and her calm demeanor when she cut through vegetables and meats. I caught her tasting her broths and salsas and closing her eyes in satisfaction and elation. I snuck photos when she cackled. Her mouth wide, her cheeks pink and her head swung back.

I created a frame out of vines, leaves, and fallen twigs. With a stepladder and determination, I made a backdrop against the brick wall of the house, big enough for Mami and my stepmom to fit into. I took photos of them in the frame. Both of them in their t-shirts and sweatpants. I took photos of my stepsisters. I shouted at them about being super models and super-heroes, but mostly super. I wanted them to know I was growing fond of them. I asked my stepmom to take a photo of me and Mami. We matched. I was wearing a pink baggy t-shirt as a dress and Mami had pink sweatpants on. I smiled on accident as I looked up at her and saw pieces of me. Here was my lineage and my stubbornness and those moments when I laughed so loud my face turned a bright red. There we were. Both of us, brilliant and hopeful, lucky enough to be on this planet at the same time, and we caught it in one photograph.

TAME THE COYOTES

Rocio was invisible because she wished to be invisible. It was that easy. She disappeared into nothing. Not even a ghost or a trickle of rainwater before it gets sent back into the atmosphere. She lived in a small town overrun by the color brown. Sepia houses. Cedar roads. Pecan trees with no leaves. Thick cracked dirt in backyards. She dreamt of the town turning into a giant pile of dust. Fire ants could take over. Colonize without remorse. The ants could transform the dusty town into a monarchy. No outsiders would think to ask any questions. The town had splotches of color because of Catholicism. Floral shrines to La Virgen de Guadalupe and San Miguel decorated the sides of tan homes. Jesus and his cross hung in gold on the front door of every home.

Rocio's body grew with intensity. One moment, she was taller than her mother. A giant above both of her Abuelas. Another moment, her hair grew past her hips. She grew hair on her upper lip, under her arms, on her knuckles. Her hips had constant bruises from corners she never suspected could betray her. Anger overcame her when older men tried to touch her long hair or question her about her age. Her answers switched between "too young for you" and "none of your god damn business." Queerness was a constant. She knew by the way she quivered and clenched her fists when a beautiful being walked past her and left behind their salty musk. She found attraction in crooked noses and big brown eyes with long eyelashes.

Every Sunday, in the stuffy church, the priest rubbed at his brow, begging the women not to give into lust. The church was packed with all of the women in town. It was an excuse for them to dress in colorful two-piece suits and lush veils. The lust lesson was repeated to them every week because of the two women who ran away together. The priest called them lesbian renegades. Rocio knew the two women would never return and she was happy for them. The women kneeled and prayed in silence. The priest was too exhausted from his own personal prayers, so there was no singing that Sunday. No Body or Blood of Christ. Rocio rolled her eyes at the petty priest and bit her tongue to feel the satisfying sting of her teeth.

Invisibility came as an impulse to live in peace from the eyes of men, even if for an hour. As an invisible entity, Rocio shed her clothes, climbed the naked trees of her brown town and listened in on the neighborhood gossip. The women spoke about divinity and sensuality. Divinity was unreachable and with that they'd be untouchable. Two of the women said they could do it. The others admitted they needed to feel the warmth of another body next to them. In her invisible state, Rocio watched the sun turn her town into a golden city. Short rectangles glistening in dust. When the sun set, it was as though the town disappeared into a void.

Rocio woke up in her bed, no longer invisible. She sat on different pecan tree branches and waved at the women in the neighborhood as they passed by. She told them if they wished to be invisible, they could pleasure themselves for as long and as hard as they wanted. Invisible women aren't seen or heard. Many of the women rushed past her. Some looked her in the eye and said thank you.

After the golden hour, Rocio wished to be invisible and so she was. She sneaked toward every house in town looking into windows. Many of the women were missing. She wondered how many women she walked past, but saw nothing and felt nothing. In celebration, she masturbated in the middle of town, next to the statue of a man with a missing face. No one knows how he got there, but he couldn't watch her if he tried. She looked into outer space and softened. She came and saw an exploding star behind her eyes. She saw purples, pinks, yellows, all a shimmer in the pools of her eye.

Every night, Rocio checked the neighborhoods. More and more women went missing. Everyone showed up in the morning, so there was nothing to be alarmed about. It tickled her to see more and more women gone after sunset. The men in their lives wandered into bars at night and sometimes into the bigger city, and they never questioned the quiet.

On the seventh night of the disappearances, the women could be heard. Howls, moans, screams, soft sighs of relief, and cackles. Frightened men with sleep residue on their eyes woke up to the thunderous sounds.

In the morning, the men called for a town meeting next to the faceless statue. They started teams of two. They assigned patrols at the edge of the town. Their objective was to tame the coyotes. Rocio followed one of the teams in the dark on their first night of patrolling. They were quiet behind white bandanas and tan clothes. They discussed shooting first, asking questions later. Then, they talked about Sunday's football game.

Rocio ran back into town and wished herself visible. She found something to wear and tore it off of a clothesline. Men walked past her and asked her why she was out so late. She ignored them and continued running until she got home. She locked the door behind her and knew what was coming next. The howls. They happened again. The cackles. The screaming. The moaning. Rocio changed into black tights and a black dress. She covered her face with black lace and a black baseball cap. She wandered into the street listening for the screaming. It surrounded her. Once the booming sound stopped, Rocio exhaled.

On the fourth night of the screams, Rocio heard gunshots in the distance. Her stomach dropped. She couldn't breathe. Vertigo hit and she fell to the ground. A wounded woman emerged in the morning. Her name was Elena. She was shot in the stomach and bled out overnight. Rocio went to the funeral with hot tears lining her face. All of the women attending wore red gowns they sewed for each other over the course of invisibility. They prayed for Elena and lit a white candle for her. Rocio left her rosary behind for Elena to have in the afterlife.

After the burial, Rocio asked all of the women to meet in the center of town. They toppled the faceless man and dumped him into an empty field with pale yellow grass. They whispered to each other. They didn't want to tell the men the truth. They were afraid the machistas would try and coopt invisibility and use it in the ways men like them warp anything beautiful. They picked a safe house. They chose Doña Guadalupe's house. They assigned shifts. They placed claw bathtubs in the backyard of the new safe house. Doña Guadalupe knew a thing or two about silence. She allowed the women into her home. She was delighted in the company and the chisme. The women cooked for each other. They bathed each other if they couldn't do it on their own. They read in silence until it was time to stand on guard. The claw bathtubs were filled in with hot water, rose petals, and lavender. Magnolia oil and lotus oil coated the invisible women. They hid in their temporary beds.

When it was time for the howls to erupt, Rocio and the women stood around the perimeter of the house in their red gowns. When the men with guns passed by, the women claimed to hear nothing. The women became so good at lying, the men started to question whether they heard anything at all.

THE MERMAID

Mayra waited until she could hear her dad snoring and white noise from her mom's phone. Mayra stuffed her backpack with essentials. Water. Granola bars. Chocolate. Grapes. A flashlight and batteries. An extra sweater and a scarf. Her parents grounded her because she got a C in Algebra on her report card and because she scoffed at her mom when she threatened to take her phone away. They took the phone and hid it somewhere in their room. It was too risky to go in there and retrieve her beloved phone. Mayra tiptoed passed their room and passed their dog, Gremlin. She put her finger over her mouth as she looked Gremlin in his suspicious eyes. She pushed her backpack through the doggie door and then squirmed through it as quiet as she could. Her heart was going so fast, she thought she was going to faint. This was her first time doing this. She tiptoed away from the house and into the next block. Then the next. There was someone across the street in a bright yellow raincoat. The shadowy figure of a person held their hand up to Mayra as a greeting. Mayra waved back.

The mermaid shimmered under the moonlight. Her silver hair clung onto her naked body. Her tail was long and silver, it wriggled behind her like the tail of a rattlesnake. The moon was big and full and illuminating the water. The glistening sea was calm. On top of a colony of exposed rocks, she perched and finished biting into the belly of a scorpionfish with her sharp and skinny teeth. Her midnight snack was interrupted. A frantic young girl ran from the forest and to the shoreline. She was breathing fast and telling herself *calm down calm down calm down*, then the girl stopped and watched the mermaid as she lingered for a moment, only to disappear as the girl squinted to get a better look at what she just saw.

The mermaid floated on her back and watched the stars above her spin. According to her sister, the stars are the souls of the dead. Ancestral cells burning in the form of twinkling specks in the night sky. Her species was dying. Faster and faster. Younger and younger. The mermaid was next in line to die. It started with a black tongue. Then, cloudy eyes. It moved onto numb arms then, forgetting where she was, having outbursts of rage which ended with her wrecking her precious coral and anemone garden. It was an inevitable demise. In the middle of the night, she snuck away from her village and swam to the shore. She wanted to see one more human before she perished. She was perplexed at their audacity for living in a finite world as though it wouldn't one day be engulfed by the ocean. The sea knows how much more it can take before it turns her back on these strange and beautiful self-obsessed creatures.

She wondered if she should go take a closer look at the girl. Should she eat her? Should she drown her? She decided against it. If she went over and played with her, the girl's adult interpretation would most likely be that it was a dream or her imagination overcompensating for how alone she felt. The mermaid found sand dollars and shells and dropped them into her net. She collected smooth stones and shining pieces of glass from the ocean floor. She had a knack for creating art out of the items she procured. It calmed her. She created intricate murals in the middle of the night, never in spaces where a human could see. Tonight was different. The mermaid made mandala patterns in the sand with her stones. Her spit made objects glow, so each stone went into her mouth and then into the mural. This piece was glowing geometric patterns which looked like an ancient language dedicated to the moon. The girl wandered over to the art, her mouth open in awe. She picked up some of the stones and stacked them into her pocket. She waved with both her hands and ran toward the mermaid. The girl embraced the mermaid as though they knew each other. The mermaid could see that she had chunky streaks of gray in her hair. The mermaid thought of silver fish swimming in the black of her full head of hair. The mermaid could smell the stench of sour sweat coming from the girl, as though she was running for her life. The girl looked at the mermaid and softly mouthed *Please help me*. The mermaid eyed a seagull, dunked into the water and leaped after it. When she caught the bird, she took it back to the shore. The girl asked if the mermaid heard her. She nodded. *Can you please help me?* The mermaid shook her head no. The girl asked if she was a mermaid. The mermaid nodded yes. She took the seagull by the head and broke its neck. She bit into the belly of the bird and blood soaked her face and chest. Her saliva mixed with the blood made the streaks of blood take on a glowing aura. The girl's eyes grew wide and she asked, *Do you eat people?* The mermaid shook her head no. This was a lie. Mermaids used to eat humans. They used to offer human bones as part of seasonal rituals to the gods below the ocean floor. Those were the ancient times, when humans were afraid of most things, before they were at their most destructive. The mermaid watched as the girl broke down to cry into her palms.

The girl said she ran away from home because she got into a big fight with her mom and dad. A strange man followed her throughout the night. He followed her into convenience stores, he followed her block after block and into people's backyards. He watched her as she hid behind cars and tried to hide in the dark. He continued finding her, smiling at her, telling her she should let him keep her. Then, she found herself in the forest. The strange man with long strides continued behind her. He called on her. *Little girl. Little girl. Look at me.* The girl didn't know where else to go, then she heard the ocean. She sniffled and tears rolled gently down her small round face. Her face shimmered under the moonlight. The mermaid never had children because she couldn't stand the thought of dying while they were still young. The mermaid patted the girl on the head and gave her some shards of glass from her net. The mermaid leaped back into the water. She was craving starfish. She plucked two unsuspecting plump treats from the sand and came back to the surface. Maybe the girl could eat one?

A man was now with the girl. The strange man. He was tall and graying. He wore a bright yellow rain jacket. The girl cried quietly. The mermaid watched as the man placed his hand on the girl's shoulder. The girl looked out into the water. The man covered her mouth. He tried to drag her away from the shore and back into the forest. The girl fought back and kicked the strange man in the shins and then she high kicked him in the groin. The girl caught a glimpse of the mermaid. The mermaid slithered closer to them. She propped her upper body out of the water, gave the girl a signal to cover her eyes. The girl took the shards of glass in her pocket and tried to shove them into the man's eyes. The mermaid lunged herself at the strange man. The man saw the mermaid and said What the fuck? The girl ran toward the water. The mermaid bit into the strange man's neck and ripped it open. The man gurgled his hot blood as the mermaid chewed on the chunk in her mouth. The girl covered her mouth, shocked and relieved at the same time. She scream-cried and then fell to her knees. The mermaid grabbed the man's oily hair and dragged him into the water.

She swam with his dying body into the pitch-black ocean with the sound of her gills bursting with bubbles. She listened to the whales singing to each other in the darkness. Some of them were mourning. Some of them were singing their calves to sleep. A calm came over her. She tugged at his head and ripped it from his body. She took the severed strange man to her destroyed garden. She bit into his face, eating his eyes and his nose. She pulled at his small intestines and marveled at the length. She ripped him limb from limb. She dug into his chest with her teeth and yanked out his heart. She left it as an offering to the old gods, the ones who forgot about her and her village.

The mermaid swam back to the shore. The girl was crying into her knees. The mermaid gave her the signal to sleep. She put stones in her mouth and then around the girl in a circle. The girl, in the fetal position, tossed and turned throughout the night. The mermaid watched over her until the sun started to rise. The pink sky and sunlight enveloped her iridescent skin. She laid on her back as the tide washed over her and then away from her body. The girl woke up, watched the mermaid, and wondered where she was born. What was she like as a child? How long has she been alive? What do mermaids name each other? The girl felt a light tap on her shoulder.

Mayra?! Oh my god, why did you sneak out? I was looking for you all night.

It was her dad.

All of this felt like a dream to Mayra. She touched her dad's face and then cried into his shoulder and said sorry. *I'm so sorry, daddy.* Snot and hot tears filled her dad's shirt. Her dad carried her all the way to the car, past the beach houses and the sand. In the backseat, under a heavy blanket, Mayra thought about the mermaid.

Was any of this real?

The mermaid swam back to her village. She told her sister about the girl and the strange man in her garden. Her sister decided to believe that the disease was getting worse. The mermaid hugged her sister and told her she was very wrong, the girl was real and the strange man was real.

The mermaid was exhilarated and rejuvenated by the final decisions she made in this life, even as the Ancient Octopus of the Underworld came to her the next night with beady yellow eyes all over its body. It led her deeper into the trenches, closer and closer to the Underworld. All the mermaid hoped was that the girl would remember her, always. She hoped the sea would remind the girl that sometimes, bad men drown and that's the most justice the world will give.

COSMOS, OKLAHOMA

The Baptism

The pastor cuts Raquel's head on accident with a crucifix ring from his middle finger. Submerged in the holy water, her blood adds drama to the debacle. She was convert number one hundred. This meant she was to be the final member of the church. The congregation showed up to celebrate the centenary baptism with a potluck and homemade confetti. They made her a crown of fossils, pinecones, honeysuckle vines, and wildflowers to wear after she was saved. Raquels's getting baptized because she's had enough of living in a tourist trap town that smells like chicken shit. The man who was nearly drowning her in holy water was charismatic enough. He made grand conjectures of time travel and astral projection into heaven. She fucked him in a rock quarry where trilobite fossils bring small conventions of enthusiasts in the spring. It was summer and Raquel was in a teeny yellow bikini, floating on a donut, almost asleep, when she spotted him. He looked like a wizard with a salt and pepper beard, long wavy hair, and a heavily tattooed body. He was speaking in tongues or something and then she caught his eye.

Raquel is in a white gown and all she can think about is how cold the water is. Did she wear the right kind of bra? Her nipples were very hard and she was very cold. The pastor holds her down with his right hand, his white suit sleeve getting soaked and now rust colored with a hint of her blood. He's screaming scripture and it sounds like warped slow motion to Raquel. She can't hold her breath any longer so she grabs the pastor's hand, pushes it away and then leaps up gasping for air. An onlooker is pointing at the water. Raquel started her period, or a horror version of it. The blood is trickling down and won't stop. It has filled the holy water tub. Her gown is now a rusty pastel pink and she smells like sundrenched metal. Raquel can't read the pastor's face because he's wearing sunglasses. She gives him a thumbs up as if to say the baptism worked. She steps out of the tub, bows to the crowd, and then runs for the bathroom. In the mirror, she sees she's lined in light streaks of her blood. Raquel smooshes her lips together then covers her mouth with her hands because she wants to laugh. She wants to go back out and cackle like a newfound witch.

The Rift

In the town of Cosmos, Oklahoma, the earth gets ripped open in the center of Main Street. The sky goes yellow, tornado yellow, and the wind screams through faulty windows. Coyotes rush to the site and howl like sirens. A rushing river of glittering neon blue liquid exposes itself in the rift and the town trembles. Small earthquakes shift houses and daycares and the hospital. Every twenty-one days, it stays open for thirty-three seconds and then disappears.

Cosmos has the highest number of cults in all of the country. For the past seven years, they come and go, depending on the affiliation to the end-of-days. Doomsday cults tend to last anywhere from a few months to a year before they walk into the river. No one has technically made it into the river, because getting too close to the rift means getting obliterated into a gush of blood and then beams of bending lights. It's breathtaking for a moment. A miniature aurora borealis sparkling from their deaths. Blink and an entire cult is annihilated. The city council has posted street signs and made billboards warning people not to go near the river. They urge everyone to go inside when the rift opens. They run TV ads with the slogan, "The rift is the Earth's business. Abide the law. Stay inside. Don't commit suicide."

Welcome to Cosmos

Anaya Montoya, local journalist, tornado chaser, and secret tour guide for the magical river, has a monthly column where she covers the new religious groups who come through the town of Cosmos. She doesn't call them cults in her articles anymore because of the implications of the word. Cult implies manipulation, an egotistical leader, potential money-laundering, and sexual exploitation. While all of these were true depending on the leadership, the cults are her primary readership in town. She treats it more like a "Welcome to Cosmos" column. For her work, she interviews the leaders. Some of these leaders, she's never seen in person. One of them was a hologram of a rat. Another sent in a jar filled with what she concluded had to be semen. She threw it away and a band of raccoons found it in the dumpster and now have it in one of their lairs. Once, she had to conduct an interview in an empty room with a mirror facing her, blocking her view of the leader. She was only allowed a pen and paper to jot down the nonsensical scripture.

Cult Eleganza

The town became a circus of specialized religions, spinning themselves as persecuted peoples or as the ONE religion that had the key to eternal life. Eternal life could mean coming back as a new person, life after life, or meeting God in a spaceship. Every group has a uniform of sorts. Hooded robes, bath robes, jumpsuits, monochrome outfits to show who they belonged to. Some wore home-made clothing and let their hair grow to the ground. There was one group that shaved their heads and painted them blue all the way down to their noses.

The Sacrifices

It was amusing until it wasn't. Anaya grew tired of being lonely in a bustling town of fanatics and followers. Then, there were the sacrifices. Three people were sliced open. Their hearts were carefully presented on one of the corner curbs where the rift opens. The bodies were found buried on top of inhabited graves. They were placed on their backs and their bellies were filled with amethysts, shards of glass, and fossils. Their eyes were gouged and replaced with robin eggs. They were blindfolded in red thread. Their bodies were painted red, their hands had gold nails jammed into the palms, and their feet were bound with gold scarves. Each person had a bullet wound at the center of their forehead which was then filled with honey.

Investigative journalists, amateur and otherwise, swarmed the town. They were looking for answers to these murders, they were looking for missing family members, they were looking to write the next viral article that would drown them in clout. Anaya was annoyed by the journalists who came through and gawked at the permanent residents of Cosmos as though they needed pity. Before the rift, before the cult, and before the murders, everything was fine by her. It just got boring sometimes. Boring was normal. Her most sensationalized stories at the time covered cow runaways with cute *WANTED* posters at the center of the article and the annual dog pageant which caused a scuffle downtown because the owner of Gazpacho the Pomeranian contested that the judging was rigged. Anaya could tell when the out-of-town journalists assumed she was stupid or didn't know any better about life beyond Oklahoma. To the judgmental journalists, Anaya replied to their inquiries with lies on lies. To the nice journalists, Anaya pointed them toward the folks who could give them more information on whatever they were looking into.

The Wizard

Raquel is one of three women who stays by the wizard's side. She's basically a homemaker at this point. She washes his clothes and cleans up after he eats. She takes any psychedelic he gives her and she sees neon saints and fuzzy cryptids as she hangs bedsheets to dry. The wizard's number one is Daisy, she's a friendly young woman with a squeaky voice. She's a dependable gossip with a heart of gold. His number two is Celina, who cooks as though it comes from her soul and who sings like a fucking angel. Then, there's Raquel. She's clever, hot, and obedient. She knows how to tease the wizard in ways that make him feel young again. She keeps his house clean and she's taken stellar photos for the group's social media. The women get along fine. They work well together in keeping the wizard happy and keeping their churches worshipping schedule organized and consistent. The wizard always said that the key to keeping followers is charisma, the promise of a better life after death, and consistency. The wizard sees himself as a renewed version of someone like Jesus, not Jesus himself, just someone like him.

The wizard is planning a gigantic party before the next rift opens. He wants to be sent off blitzed out of his mind before he jumps into the rift. He has urged the church members not to follow him. He claims he will come back to them in their dreams with a specific message from paradise for each person.

The party is being held outside and all of town will be invited. The theme is "Ethereal Beings from Outer Space" and nudity is highly encouraged. Flyers have been posted all over town.

A New Kind of Sacrifice

Another sacrifice happened. The body was dragged down the middle of Main Street. Their heart was missing and their body was painted gold. Their eyes were missing and filled in with white candle wax. Coyotes were picking at the body until Martha Delgado shot at them with the revolver she kept at her side. The coyotes scattered and the body twitched violently. Martha called Anaya right away and Anaya sped downtown. The sound of bones cracking echoed down the empty street. Martha stepped back and then ran to her shop. She locked the door and watched as the body stood upright. Some of the skin was torn away and flapping in the breeze. The face smiled at her before being launched into the sky. Anaya hit the body with her car.

Trilobite Confessional

The wizard prepared for his goodbye party by swimming in the trilobite quarry and listening to his heartbeat and breathing underwater. He had no need for this vessel anymore. He imagined his skin peeling off of him like a snake, then his exposed muscles underneath being ripped away by piranhas, his organs scattering like meaty confetti and floating to the surface of the quarry. He watched as he turned into bones that rattled like wind chimes, picked up in a tornado and then flung into different parts of the planet. This brought a feeling of hope.

What if there's nothing after this?

What if there's everything after this and I become a part of it?

The Creature

Anaya watches as the golden body stands upright and walks toward the trailer park. Martha steps out of her shop and with trembling hands, she shoots at the body. She misses and then grazes the body's shoulder with her next shot. The body keeps walking. Anaya and Martha run behind it and get close enough to smell it. It smells like sulfur. The body turns around and Martha shoots it in the head. A yellow substance bursts from the back of its head. The face smiles at them with dark yellow teeth and bile pouring from the crevices of its teeth. The body lunges at Martha and bites her belly. The body's tongue stretches out in a loop, proboscis-like, and punctures through Martha's belly. The tongue suctions out blood from the puncture. Anaya tries to jump on the body, but it grabs her by the neck and tosses her in the air. Anaya can't think as her head cracks on the ground and her body spins onto the gravel. She can feel the warmth of the blood from the crown of her head bloom around her and soak into her hair. The commotion brings folks out of their homes, followed by screaming as they see the body, now sprouting what looks like elkhorns from the sides of its head and bony wings from its back.

The wizard walks back into town and is surprised by the crowd gathered downtown. There are men on loudspeakers claiming the end of days is upon us, finally. There are people on their knees. An ambulance wails and EMTs are trying to get through the crowd to get to someone who is apparently bleeding out. The wizard sprints around the crowd and finds a gap toward the front. He sees the creature, which looks like a giant demonic moth. It's oddly divine. The wizard rushes toward Anaya and picks her up. He runs with her through the crowd. The crowd moves like a school of silverfish around him and Anaya. He whispers to her that she has to go into the rift. She has to see what's on the other side. Anaya is slipping in and out of consciousness and she's terrified. She's scared that she's going to die. She's sad that she has to die. The wizard places her gently in the center of Main Street. He runs from the center and tries to get the crowd to move back. Then, an earthquake. The wizard runs away from the crowd and toward his house. People fall over each other as they continue to gawk at the creature. The rift opens and Anaya bursts into blood and then, a beautiful neon light show. Others fall into the rift and spray blood and then light. Screams follow as the creature becomes curious and flies overhead. The creature is more interested in the wizard who is running alone. The creature knows that the man is scared. The creature flies above the wizard and then jumps down on top of him to stomp on the man with its newly grown hooves. The creature stomps the wizard's head in and then proceeds to suck out the blood through the top of his head.

When the wizard doesn't show up to his party, Raquel wears her crown and runs around the party as though she's the new leader. She proclaims that the party must go on and once everyone's asleep, either the wizard or the creature will come for them with a message from above.

MORNING OF THE TEETH

The exorcism started as the sun rose over the desert mountains. Alejandra twitched and spasmed on the black and white tile of the church bathroom. Dust devils spun in the parking lot and any witness could see the lights flicker inside the church as the sky darkened the morning. The exterior of the church was a replica of the Ringebu Stave Church. The Priest input his opinion on what the church should look like. He emphasized his beliefs in God as a relationship of pain and elements of euphoria. He wanted the building to reflect that. Every Sunday, he was delighted to see the nervous faces of attendants before they shuffled in. He wanted them to look up at the red tower and ask themselves if they would ever make it past the sky after they decay. Inside, the church was filled with gold-framed gloss portraits of saints. There was a gigantic white marble tub filled with holy water next to the confessional. A daunting crucifix, which was said to have bled at one point in its existence, watched down on the praying crowd Sunday mornings.

Alejandra's mother, Estela, had grown concerned because Alejandra spent the day prior screaming without an explanation. High-pitched screeching and sometimes deep wailing moans were coming out of her daughter. Alejandra answered none of her questions and didn't eat or succumb to sleep. She screamed until her mother could no longer stand the sound. Estela carried Alejandra over her shoulder, into the town's church. Alejandra continued screaming as they stepped inside. She crawled in between the pews and felt the cracks in the floor. She put her ear to the floor and heard a pulse under the earth. With earnest intent, she listened and then the heartbeat put her to sleep.

The Priest suggested an exorcism. This would be his third one. A trinity. He cracked his knuckles and chills overtook him. He was thrilled to perform another exorcism and on such short notice. He gawked at Alejandra who fell asleep underneath the crucifix with Jesus cloaked in gold silk. As The Priest reached out to touch her head, Alejandra woke up and started to scream. The Priest scoffed and asked the creature in the church if this was some form of a joke. The creature could only be seen out of the corner of his eye, but the smell of burnt hair guaranteed his presence. The creature whispered and The Priest turned to try and see what spoke to him, but the creature dematerialized into dancing dust.

Alejandra crawled away and hid in the bathroom. The Priest found her behind a curtain of St. Michael. He placed his hand on her shoulder and started praying. As she wriggled without any control of her body, a memory flashed into her: the time she unearthed a lizard after having put it to rest three days prior. Maybe the lizard was getting revenge. Then, there was the woman she saw at the end of the street who seemed to be screaming, but Alejandra heard nothing. Maybe Alejandra was a manifestation of her voice. Sweat poured from Alejandra and her teal dress became soaked in her salt. A vibrant and cartoonish blood red cardinal bounced out of her mouth. The very round bird flew at The Priest, then in a circle, then back toward Alejandra. In drenched feathers, the cardinal perched on her forehead as her little breaths were left unheard by the commotion coming from the mouth of The Priest. His sweat was dripping onto the tile. His face was red. The motions of his tongue were alien. A gurgling language along with the spit bubbles to match.

Alejandra's main interest was ponies. Short-legged, four-legged, with silky hair and goofy teeth. She loved Quarter ponies and Shetland ponies. She loved them so much, she made a birth certificate with a majestic name in case someone ever gifted her one: Queen Reginald Lavender. Her second interest was death. Estela told Alejandra near-death experience stories. There was the one time at the laundromat. The static inside was so intense, she thought her insides were going to boil. Then the time in the swimming pool when she was alone. Something grabbed onto her foot and tickled her belly. She made it up for air just in time. Her mother claimed to have almost died eleven times. Alejandra found this fascinating and wondered how many times she would almost die in her lifetime. Alejandra thinks her first near-death experience was three Sundays ago. The sky was red from a blustering desert day. The wind nudged Alejandra over a curb where she landed on her knees so hard, she tore open her tights. As she looked up, a black goat stood on its hind legs and laughed.

The reality of their new life in town was this: Estela met and followed a man who was sweet and caring at first, but his thirst for violence became transparent as the relationship went from a matter of months into years. She followed him for three years. The move was his decision. Estela almost died at his fists multiple times. Alejandra saw the state of her mother and wondered what she saw in her dreams as she twitched. How could she fall asleep with an insect of a man lying next to her? She imagined her mother as a Luna moth with torn wings flailing in the bed and she saw the violent man as a fire ant, waiting to sting.

When Alejandra smiled, exposed gums shimmered where her two front teeth should have been. Sugar had decayed two of her molars and then there was the violent man. He pulled at her two front teeth as soon as he became annoyed by her screaming. He jammed his thumb and pointer finger into her mouth. Alejandra trembled and tried her best to wriggle away as he picked her up by the neck. He pulled at the teeth harder and harder until they started to budge, then, her teeth became his. He kept them in his wallet and walked away from the situation.

The blood dribbling from her mouth became little streams down her belly and her skinny brown legs.

As the exorcism continued, she thought about her sixth birthday and the confetti on the asphalt the morning after. She kept the confetti in a shoebox and separated the pieces by color. She carried different colors with her like a bruja carries crystals. Blue pieces of confetti meant the sky was watching over her. Pinks meant she could only speak to those she loves. Red meant blood and healing. She rubbed the red confetti over her scabs and asked for her scars to be hers and hers alone. The violent man had never touched her, until the morning of the teeth.

The screaming only started because of a nightmare. Creatures with inside-out skin followed Alejandra in the forest. Their hot labored breathing stuck to her neck and her spine. She could hear their bones rattling and the organs squishing together as they followed her down a path that only seemed to go around and around until she finally came across river water. Alejandra heard the creatures gasping and panting. One-two-three. One-two-three. One-two-three. She looked at her feet in the water and a thick red sludge took over. As the river dried, a body appeared. It was a faceless person. Alejandra tried to shake the person awake and it grabbed at her hands, forcing her reach through the belly button of its body. Sharp points cut through Alejandra's palms and fingers. The skin of the body opened up, peeling away limb from limb and was taken by the breeze like a paper bag. It left behind amethyst crystal clusters. Alejandra reached for them and salivated. She threw a few clusters into the forest for the creatures and they accepted the offering by turning their skin back to normal. A goat, a pony, and a short gray creature chewed on the amethyst together. The crunching of the crystals sounded like wind chimes. As the creatures finished their meals, another body appeared in front of them. A bloated corpse with flies circling around it. It called for help, so Alejandra reached toward the body with her hand. As it grabbed at her, the face was her mother's. Alejandra woke up screaming.

The Priest poured holy water on Alejandra's body until her hands were pruned and her hair was matted to the tile. He screamed at the demon to go. He screamed at Alejandra to come back to the light. He saw this impure and defective body and felt pity, excitement, and fear. The exorcism finalized as the sun set. Alejandra continued to scream, but her voice started to go hollow. The Priest took Estela aside and gave her another option. He wanted to send Alejandra into the forest with other children like her. If Alejandra was susceptible to spirits, forest spirits were the easiest to tame. The creature of the church let out a murmur of joy. It agreed with The Priest. Send the child off. The Priest handed Estela a flyer for a vigil and asked for the most recent photograph of Alejandra so they could mourn her soul.

Estela did not bring a photo of Alejandra. She left Alejandra at home. Alejandra had finally given in to sleep again and dreamt of short ponies racing together in lavender fields. Estela attended the vigil and her gut went in knots. Candles with photographs of babies and children were lined up in front of the church. Parents knelt and scraped their palms together begging the sky to lead their kin into heaven. Others laid on their bellies and cried into the grass, earthworms feasting on their salt. Then, there were the unexplained photographs. Estela didn't recognize some of the children in the vigil. Were they new in town too? Where had they come from? The children, dressed in white gowns, were led through the back door of the building. The pre-teens held the babies in their arms. One infant was strapped into a white stroller. The older children watched from the red tower of the church. They watched as their parents wailed for them as though they were really dead.

Once the mourning vigil was over, the priest led the children into a white van. Estela followed in her green Sentra. She was not incognito by any means. She drove close to the van, too afraid she would lose the kids. The van drove toward Hyde Memorial State Park. It drove deeper and deeper into the winding roads and finally pulled over to park. Estela went further up the road and parked on the side, sprinting back toward the van. The Priest led the children out of the van, one by one. He led them through a side trail where wreaths decorated the branches of the dying trees at the entrance of the trail. Estela followed and noticed the tree-tops drooped down, creating a tunnel. The children kept pace with The Priest. The last child noticed Estela behind them, but continued to follow the other children. As the tunnel ended, three stained-glass structures erupted from the soil. A crimson pyramid, a blue door, and a green geometric structure that reached into the clouds. The Priest crawled into the pyramid and the children followed. As they crawled, soggy mud drenched their white robes, and hands from under the earth grabbed at their feet and their hair. One of the babies was snatched into the earth as they continued their trek. The children kept their focus. They were going to heaven. They were going to heaven. They were promised. The infant in the white stroller stayed behind and when Estela ran to grab the child, something else had already gotten a hold of it.

In town, Alejandra woke up alone. She shuffled around the house and made herself some chamomile tea. The urge to scream had diminished until she saw the violent man sitting in the living room. He asked where her mother had gone to. A shrug and limbs shaking. Alejandra searched for exit strategies. The kitchen window. The doggie door. The bathroom door could be locked and she could wiggle through the sliding window. The violent man stood up. Alejandra placed her hand in front of him, signaling STOP. The violent man suddenly collapsed and foamed at the mouth. Something grabbed Alejandra's head from behind and pushed her toward the violent man. His body still, the entity grabbed Alejandra's right hand and shoved it into the violent man's throat. Vomit erupted from the man and Alejandra couldn't help but cry. She grabbed through the warmth. It was a photograph of her mother as a child. Alejandra recognized the smile and the curly hair with white streaks in the bangs. Alejandra went into the throat of the man again and there were dozens of photographs. All of her mother as a child.

Estela ran as fast as she could through the drooping trees. The trees turned orange and yellow behind her as she made it through the tunnel. She drove back into town, screaming, her stomach burning with regret for doing nothing. She thought about Alejandra and what she would do if she ever lost her. She wiped her tears and imagined the town church burned into ash. She parked her car in front of the church, waiting on The Priest.

The children had been given to the forest spirits. They now had the ability hear the trees and the roots and the animals murmuring to each other, whispering about another kind of history no human could ever know. It made the children have a tinge of green to their skin. They become the voices and giggles overheard while walking a forest trail alone.

When nightfall came and The Priest was done leading the children into the forest, he returned to the church energized and ready to hear confessions from the townspeople. The creature of the church watched The Priest slick back his hair and crack his knuckles. He sat inside the confessional and waited for someone to say anything. Estela sat on the other side.

"I know what you did to the children."

The creature watched The Priest's immediate escape from the confessional. Estela repeated herself.

"I saw what you did to the children."

With The Priest no longer there, a small voice replied. A young girl.

"Forgive me Father, for I have sinned."

Estela replied, "Wh-what can I help you with child?"

"I keep imagining the death of a man. I don't know who he is, but somebody left his photograph under my pillow. I see him in my dreams and every time he shows up, I find a way to kill him. I've shoved him off a cliff. I've watched him drown. I have seen him gasp for air and all I could do was step on his throat. I don't know who he is, and I can't stop."

"Does this man scare you?"

"Yes."

"Can you show me the picture?"

Small hands and a gentle nudge at the feet of Estela.

"The man in the photo can't hurt you."

"I know. He hasn't hurt me yet."

"Not yet, but he will soon and I'm so sorry. Your imagination is meant to be wild, weird, and sometimes dark. Never let that escape you. Um, go sit in the tub of holy water and lick the first page of the Bible before you go to bed."

A giggle and then the sound of a body dunking itself into water. Estela stayed in the confessional until she could hear the footsteps leave the church. She used to lick the pages of the Bible when she was a girl because she couldn't read yet. She used to tell her mother she knew the Bible better than any man because the words were inked into her tongue. She was five.

Estela stepped out of the confessional and searched for The Priest. He had gone up to the tower to watch people tend to the tombstones plotted behind the church. Estela ran up the spiral stairs until she saw the back of The Priest's head. She thought about bashing his head into the wall. She thought about lighting him on fire.

"There's nothing you can do about the kids. They're gone. They've been given away."

"To what? The forest spirits?"

"You should take your daughter out of this town. They like unusual children."

"So, you're going to continue doing this?"

"It's tradition. It's a way for parents to feel like their children are guaranteed a spot in heaven."

"What about you? Where will you end up?"

"In this town. In this church. I am a man of God and gospel. I never lied about where the children go. I only speak the truth. God approves it. He speaks to me. He's here. He's with us now."

The creature of the church stretches his limbs and extends his body in front of The Priest for the first time. His claws stretch and caress The Priest's face, poking into his eye socket, clasping onto his eye. Then, he goes for the other eye. He curls in his claws until they both pop out. He slurps on both eyes and whispers to The Priest. It's incoherent, but The Priest knows. Estela only sees the aftermath. The Priest's face is pouring blood and he's wailing.

Estela's chest is heavy as she runs down the spiral staircase and out of the church. The creature of the church watches as she stumbles out. Estela's only urge is to speed home to Alejandra. Alejandra's outside with a suitcase and a stack of books. She's wearing a white dress with a red cardinal sewn into the fabric.

"I think we need to leave, Mami."

"I think you're right."

Estela knew better than to go back into the house. She looked back at Alejandra sleeping on her luggage and her chest filled with warmth. She drove them through the pitch-black desert until she found a new town under a new pink sky where they could start over.

ACKNOWLEDGMENTS:

Thank you to my friends and family who encourage me to stay weird with my storytelling. Thank you to David, a nurturing and hot dad, a chaotic and beautiful Sagittarius, you are my love. Thanks to Ally Winslow, my media sandia. Thank you to Brigit Fraga, your art is incredible and I enjoy your crow stories so much. Thank you to Gus Amaral, for your wonderful art and friendship, I love you and Kelci so much. Thank you to Evelyn Nevarez, for letting me use your beautiful face for the cover, you inspire me every day with your Taurus discipline and love for Liam and Noah. Thank you to Meliza Bañales, one of the most giving souls I know, you are a treasure. Thank you to Alma Rosa Rivera-Castor, a beam of light and phenomenal poet, I love you friend. Shout-out to my Oklahoma homies: Rai, Valeria, Chermaine, Jenna, Eric, Allie, Natasha, Julius, and Laine. I love your humor, your vibes, your creativity. Thank you to the Corporeal crew for being angels and pushing me to dig deeper. Lidia, I love you. Finally, I want to thank my beautiful baby, Gustavo, for choosing me to mother him, I love you so much, it hurts. You make the world more whimsical and awe-inspiring. This planet is lucky to have you on it.

ABOUT THE AUTHOR:

Rios de la Luz is a queer bruja living in Oklahoma with her love and her beautiful son. She is the author of the short story collection, The Pulse between Dimensions and the Desert (Ladybox Books 2015), and the novella, Itzá (Broken River Books 2017).